EVERYBODY NEEDS A BUDDY

The Big Idea Gang

EVERYBODY NEEDS A BUDDY

By James Preller

Illustrated by Stephen Gilpin

Houghton Mifflin Harcourt

BOSTON   NEW YORK

hmhco.com

The text was set in Adobe Caslon Pro.

Library of Congress Cataloging-in-Publication Data
Names: Preller, James, author. | Gilpin, Stephen, illustrator.
Title: Everybody needs a buddy / by James Preller.
Description: Boston ; New York : Houghton Mifflin
Harcourt, [2019] | Series: The Big Idea Gang ; [2] |
Summary: Third-graders Deon, Kym, Lizzy, and Connor,
armed with Miss Zips' persuasive tips, set out to convince the
PTA to use their cash surplus to put a "buddy bench" on the
playground.
Identifiers: LCCN 2018032031| ISBN 9781328857194
(hardback) | ISBN 9781328973405 (paperback)
Subjects: | CYAC: Schools—Fiction. | Persuasion
(Psychology)—Fiction. | Friendship—Fiction. |
Playgrounds—Fiction. | BISAC: JUVENILE FICTION /
School & Education. | JUVENILE FICTION / Readers /
Chapter Books. | JUVENILE FICTION / Social Issues /
Friendship. | JUVENILE FICTION / Humorous Stories.
Classification: LCC PZ7.P915 Eve 2019 | DDC [Fic]—dc23
LC record available at https://lccn.loc.gov/2018032031

Printed in the United States of America
DOC 10 9 8 7 6 5 4 3 2 1
4500739485

*My thanks to Lorraine Preziosi,
a classroom teacher who patiently answered my
questions. Your perceptions and insights helped guide
parts of this book.*

Table of Contents

CHAPTER 1

The Best Part of the Day

For Deon Gibson, there was no debate. Only one answer could be correct. Recess was absolutely, positively, 100 percent, totally the best part of the school day. No one could convince him otherwise.

Sure, some kids liked PE best.

They were wrong.

Others kids loved math.

But again, according to Deon, those people were nuts. Sure, those math-loving students might go on to become scientists or computer wizards, but Deon didn't care.

"Recess is the best part of the school day,"

Deon claimed to anyone who'd listen at his Clay Elementary cafeteria table.

"That's just your opinion," Kym replied.

"Not opinion, fact!" Deon stated.

"Well, personally, *in my opinion*, I like reading better." Kym Park closed her eyes and smiled. "Silent, independent reading. And I love it when Miss Zips reads out loud to us. Ah, pure heaven. I could listen to her read books all day."

"Reading is okay," Deon countered. "But you have to sit still and be quiet. That's so not me. I'm the opposite. At recess, I get to run around and scream my head off. I get to see all my friends. We laugh and joke around. We play ball. Plus" —he tapped the left side of his chest—"it's good for the old ticker."

Connor O'Malley shoved a fistful of chips into his mouth. He said, "Lunschhh."

Kym swiveled her head in Connor's direction. Then she turned to Connor's twin sister, Lizzy. "What did he say?"

Lizzy O'Malley shook her head. "My brother

is trying to say 'lunch,' Kym, but Connor's face is too stuffed with food—as usual. Connor, could you please swallow your chips before speaking?"

"Shhhorry," Connor apologized, still chewing.

Deon leaned forward. "I know a guy who tried this trick where he ate ten crackers crazy fast and tried to whistle. You have like thirty seconds to do it. And I'm telling you, it's impossible—*and*

it's hysterical. Crackers were flying everywhere. It was raining Saltines!"

Kym made an *ew* face.

"Sounds disgusting," Lizzy said.

"No, trust me, it's funny," Deon said. "The crackers absorb all the water in your mouth. Then you can't whistle."

Kym frowned. "I can't whistle at all. Even without crackers."

"It's easy," Connor said. "Just put your lips together and blow." He let out a whistle that would have made a sparrow proud.

Kym furrowed her brows in concentration. She pushed out her lips to form a tight circle. She puffed out her cheeks.

And nothing happened.

Not a peep.

Not a chirp.

Not a tweet.

"Sad!" Deon snorted.

Kym's cheeks flushed pink.

"Hey, don't laugh, Deon," Lizzy said. "I bet

there's lots of things that Kym can do that you can't."

"Yeah, like math," Connor joked.

"I can do math," Deon claimed. "I just don't see the point. Two and two makes four. What more do I need to know?"

Lizzy rose to take her things to the recycling bin. She checked the wall clock. "Well, in one hundred and eighty seconds it will become your favorite time of day."

Deon looked puzzled.

"Three minutes," Lizzy said. "Sixty seconds is a minute. Sixty times three is one eighty. That's when we go outside for recess." She grinned. "See, Deon. Math isn't so bad after all. It's just a question of how you look at it."

CHAPTER 2

The Rumor

Suri Brewster started the rumor out on the playground. Small and wiry with a wild mass of black hair, Suri joined Lizzy and Kym on the swinging footbridge. The girls held on to chain railings while the bridge rattled and swayed. Connor and Deon circled underneath, groaning and moaning, pretending to be zombies . . . or killer sharks . . . or gruesome trolls . . . or something like that. The girls didn't pay much attention. They were more interested in Suri's news.

"So, like, you know my mom is treasurer for the PTA," Suri began.

Kym and Lizzy nodded. Suri had mentioned it a few dozen times already.

"Well, Mama says there's a big surplus of money," Suri claimed. She pushed her purple, pointy glasses closer to her face.

"A big surplus?" Kym asked, unsure of exactly what that meant.

"Extra money," Suri said. "Tons of it. When we changed our mascot to the Clay Elementary Dragons, we sold, like, easily a bazillion T-shirts, hats, coffee mugs, and sweatshirts with the new logo."

"A bazillion," Lizzy murmured. "That's a lot of T-shirts."

The moaning from underneath the bridge got louder. "Better run," Connor and Deon warned in ghoulish voices. Four hands reached up and rattled the bridge. "The zombies are coming for you!"

"Connor, stop!" Lizzy shushed. "We can't play zombie apocalypse every single day. It gets boring. We're trying to talk."

Deon popped up beside the bridge. "We're not boring. You're boring."

"Yeah, what he said," Connor grumbled.

Kym ignored the boys. She asked Suri, "So what are they going to do with all that money?"

"That's the amazing thing," Suri said, bouncing on her toes with excitement. "They want to buy something cool for the school!"

Connor and Deon—forgetting they were zombies, at least for the moment—climbed up on the bridge. They were interested.

"How much money does the PTA have?" Connor asked.

"I think it's easily like a thousand dollars," Suri said. "Maybe more."

"Whoa, that's a lot of George Washingtons," Deon exclaimed.

"Yeah, a thousand of them," Kym deadpanned.

"Maybe they should buy, like . . . oh, I don't know," Connor said, somewhat pitifully.

"Genius idea," Deon kidded.

"Give me a minute, I'll think of something," Connor retorted. "I know! A rocket ship for the playground!"

"They could buy an author," Kym suggested.

"An author?" Deon asked. "I didn't know authors were for sale. Where do you get them? Aisle six at Walmart?"

Kym frowned. "I mean a visit from an author. That would be good for the whole school."

"Slow down, everybody," Lizzy said. "We really don't know any details yet."

Milo Pitts, in shorts and a mustard-stained T-shirt, raced over. He paused, half listening, and yelled up. "Connor, Deon! We need two more guys to play full-court basketball!"

"Do they have to be *guys?*" Lizzy snapped back.

"Um." Milo scratched his nose. "No, I guess anybody can play."

"Well, we're busy, thanks for asking," Lizzy replied.

Suri spied a group of friends across the field. "Oh, I have to tell Sabrina the big news," she explained to Lizzy and Kym. "Talk to you later."

Suri leaped off the bridge, sprawling in the grass. She bounced up and hustled away.

"Well? You guys coming?" Milo asked.

"Gotta fly," Connor announced to the girls. "Deon and I can't turn down a game of hoops."

— CHAPTER 3 —

The Boy by the Tree

Connor started toward the basketball court with Milo at his side. He stopped to look back. Deon was trailing behind. "Let's go, Deon. We haven't got all day."

Deon had just noticed something out of the corner of his eye: a thin, small boy standing by a tree. Curious, Deon lingered to take a longer look. He told the boys, "Go on, I'll be right there." Deon bent to tie a shoelace that didn't need tying. The boy with light-brown skin stood still, his hands dangling at his sides. It struck Deon as odd, the way the boy stood so perfectly still—as if he hoped to disappear. Some animals do that.

Chameleons, rabbits, deer. If spotted by a preda-
tor, they freeze, motionless, trying to fade into
the background. They want to be . . . *unseen*.

Deon hadn't noticed the boy before. His large
dark eyes stared in the direction of the basketball court. The expression on the boy's face was
impossible to read. *Is he angry? Is he sad?* Deon
couldn't tell.

A scramble of students hooted and jostled on
the court. They took practice shots, firing balls in
the direction of a round metal hoop. *Swish, swish,*
two in a row shivered through the metal net. A
chorus of cheers was followed by an eruption of
laughter. Milo and Connor were already on the
court. They were waiting impatiently. "Deon!
Let's go. We're choosing sides now!" Amir Ka-
zemi called.

Deon glanced again at the solitary boy by the
tree. *Does he want to play? Is he any good?* Deon
almost opened his mouth, but just at that instant
the boy turned away. He kicked a stone in the dirt
and a small puff of dust rose from the ground.

"Coming!" Deon dashed toward the basketball court. "Let's do this!"

As the boys picked sides, Milo told the others that the PTA was buying a new basketball court. "Well, not a court exactly, but new backboards and rims. We deserve real nets, with rope, not these crummy ones with rusty chains," Milo noted.

Everyone was glad to hear this piece of good news.

Watching Milo get all the attention, Connor interjected, "The PTA has, like, ten thousand extra dollars, easy. They might buy a rocket ship for the playground."

"A rocket ship!" Bobby Mumford said. "We need one of those!"

Deon wasn't listening. It was all just talk. *Blah, blah, blah.* Instead he kept thinking about that boy by the tree. He had just stood there, watching. "Do you know him?" Deon asked Milo.

"Who?"

Deon tilted his head in the direction of the boy. "Him, the kid."

Milo gave a disinterested shrug. Then a ball bounded off the rim and bounced into Milo's hands. He dribbled once, twice, spry and fancy. Milo turned and hurled up a wild shot that missed everything.

"Air ball, air ball!" Bobby teased, hands cupped around his mouth. "If you keep shooting like that, you'll have a better chance of hitting a bird than making a basket."

Milo gave Bobby a friendly shove. "We'll see who's laughing by the end of the game."

Deon pounced on a rebound. He dribbled behind his back, then between his legs, and quick as a flash took it to the hole. A flick of the fingers. Nothing but net. Man, he loved playing ball. High fives all around.

The next time Deon looked up, the boy had disappeared.

Unseen, again.

CHAPTER 4

What's the Buzz?

Miss Isadora Bliss Zipsokowski was the teacher assigned to room 312. Few students attempted to say her name out loud, in fear of getting their tongues tangled. Besides, who had time for all those syllables? Instead, she was known as "Miss Zips" or, affectionately, "the Zipster." Miss Zips was very tall and very tough. She never tried to win her students' approval by going easy on them. She made her students work hard. If anyone complained, and of course some did, Miss Zips would grin and reply, "Tough cookies. I make you work because I care about you."

Bartimus Finkle once famously grumbled, "I wish you'd care less."

But he didn't mean it. Not really. Not deep down.

When students trickled in each morning, Miss Zips gave them time to settle. The kids went to their cubbies, pulled out books, talked quietly, rubbed sleep from their eyes.

On this morning, one topic moved like electricity through the room. The PTA was going to buy something terrific for the school! But that was the only thing anyone could agree on. The

more people talked, the more excited they became. And the stories grew more and more exaggerated.

Lizzy overhead a conversation by the cubbies. Amir said, "We're getting a new swimming pool, built by the same company that did the one in the middle school."

Charlie LaCroix said, "I like swimming, but I hate getting my hair wet." Charlie had a wavy blond mane. He spent long minutes before the mirror each morning carefully arranging each golden strand.

"Don't go underwater," Amir suggested. "Float like a duck. That'll keep it dry."

Lizzy interrupted, "Amir, where did you hear we're getting a swimming pool?"

The boy looked at Lizzy and shrugged. "Everybody knows. Suri told Vanessa Knox, who passed it on to Sabrina Green, who told Milo, who told me. Besides, I think I saw a pool truck in the parking lot."

Hmmm.

Next Lizzy moved to a group of kids by the bookshelves. Rosa Morales was in the middle of a story, hands gesturing wildly as she explained to Bobby Mumford, "It's going to be an entirely new playground—with all kinds of Ninja Warrior–type stuff, like on the TV show."

"I'm not sure about that," Kaylee Simmons countered. Tall and lanky, she stood with hands on her hips. "Kym told me they were paying a famous author to do writers' workshops."

"Pish, they do that every year anyway," rosy-cheeked, freckle-speckled Hayden Chipwood said. "I heard the PTA still doesn't know what to do with the extra money."

Head buzzing with rumors, Lizzy retreated to the peace and quiet of her desk. There were so many different stories flying around, like honeybees in a flower garden. She wondered which story, if any, was true.

Miss Zips had been sitting at her desk, chatting with Mr. Sanders, the classroom aide. They were sharing a bowl of grapes. At last she stood and moved to the front center of the room. And in this way Miss Zips signaled that it was time to begin the school day. "My goodness, you are all so chatty this morning. What's the buzz all about?" A dozen excited voices spoke at once. They talked about ten thousand dollars . . . fifty thousand dollars . . . swimming pools and rocket ships . . . and much more.

"Whoa, slow down," Miss Zips said, laughing. "It sounds like there are a lot of wild rumors flying around. Usually when information gets passed from person to person, we get farther and farther away from the truth."

"Like in the game telephone," Connor said.

"Exactly," Miss Zips said. "The farther a story is passed down the line, the more it changes. By the end, we don't know what's true."

"Suri told us the PTA has a surplus of cash," Kym offered.

"Ah, yes," Miss Zips said. "Suri is well informed."

"My mother is treasurer of the PTA," Suri informed the class. She pushed her pointy purple glasses closer to her face. "She's also co-chairperson of the recycling committee."

"Yes," Miss Zips said. "We're thankful for the volunteer work that so many parents do for the school."

"So what's the truth?" Amir asked. "Are we getting a swimming pool or what?"

"I wouldn't bet on it," Miss Zips said, laughing. "I don't believe the PTA has that kind of money."

In the back of the room, Charlie LaCroix felt relieved. He truly didn't like getting wet. Even warm baths made Charlie feel sorrowful. He wasn't exactly the cleanest boy in room 312.

CHAPTER 5

Chocolate Water

Deon Gibson felt distracted for the rest of the day. He took the bus home, did his homework, ate dinner (tacos, yes!), and played video games for half an hour. That's all his parents allowed, half an hour of screen time. But all the while, his mind kept flashing back to that boy by the tree. Deon pictured him in his mind. The neat brown pants, the tucked-in, buttoned-down, perfectly pressed shirt. The way the boy stood so stiffly still, ramrod straight, hands at his sides. Deon saw his light-brown skin and short, jet-black hair. He didn't know the boy's name.

There was something else that stuck with Deon. He puzzled over it, wondering. And then Deon realized what he sensed that afternoon on the playground. The boy might be very unhappy. No one explained it to Deon—he had no way of being sure—but he knew in his heart it was true. The boy was sad. And the thought of it nagged at Deon like a loose tooth his tongue couldn't leave alone.

Strange as it may seem, Deon didn't have much experience with sadness. He was simply one of those happy kids. "Deon is naturally happy," his mother often explained. Deon had more friends than he could count, including one best friend, Connor O'Malley. The two of them were often together. If Deon ever felt alone—maybe Connor was away or something—Deon didn't really mind. He could always shoot baskets out on the driveway. Or knock on someone else's door. Or climb a tree. Or spy on his cats. Or practice cross-eyed faces in the mirror. Or lie on the grass watching the clouds drift overhead and feel the warm sun on his face, and smile.

Wasn't life wonderful?

But why would anyone ever feel sad at recess?

Deon honestly wasn't sure. It seemed wrong to Deon, like a crime against nature.

The next morning at school, Deon saw the boy in the hall. Deon was on his way to the bathroom, humming lightly to himself. No one was around. And then, *poof,* a door opened and the boy appeared. They walked toward each other, heading in different directions. The boy looked down, as if counting the floor tiles. Deon tried to make eye contact. It was impossible.

Deon stopped at the water fountain. He took a loud, extra-slurpy gulp.

"Mmmm, wow, that's good stuff!" Deon exclaimed to the boy. "Temperature's just right, too!"

The boy paused a moment, a little startled, as if a live chicken had suddenly raced across the hallway. No, it was only Deon Gibson, trying to be nice.

"Want some?" Deon asked, hand still on the knob. "It's chocolate flavored."

Now the boy really looked confused. The fingers of his right hand squeezed the knob of his left elbow. He stood there, perplexed, not daring to pass.

"I'm kidding." Deon flashed a big toothy smile. "But it is nice and cold!"

Not knowing what else to do, the boy ducked his head to the fountain. He took a quick sip and wiped his mouth with the back of his hand. "Yes,

very good," the boy said, stringing the words together in a sprint, as if in a hurry to finish speaking.

Yesverygood.

His crisp white shirt was tucked into his pants,
which Deon noticed were belted a little too tight.
Skinny ankles peeked out from the bottom of his
pant legs.

He wore purple socks.

He steered past Deon and headed away, mov-
ing swiftly, arms still at his sides.

"Hey," Deon called. "Hold up a minute."

The boy stopped. He turned his head to look
back over his shoulder. Every hair on his head
was perfectly in place, parted on the side. His
eyes were brown and round and full of questions.

Why me? What now?

Deon lifted a hand, let it drop. "What's your
name?"

"Dinesh Barazani," the boy replied. Again he
spoke quickly, without pausing between words,

and to Deon's ears the name came out as one long musical sound: *dineshbarazani*.

"Cool," Deon said. And after a moment, he added, "I'm Deon. Or D, or whatever."

Dinesh nodded sharply, one time, a quick downward stab of the chin. Then he walked away.

All Deon could think was: *Step one, mission accomplished*. He had made first contact with the new boy. And just as suddenly, a new thought pushed forward in Deon's brain: *Dinesh needs a buddy!*

CHAPTER 6

Meeting of the Big Idea Gang

Lizzy sat on a lawn chair in the crisp afternoon air, her knees close together, toes pressed against the ground. Connor and Kym sat to her right on an old wooden bench. Kym had a notebook on her lap, pen poised in the air. Deon leaned on an elbow, sprawled on the green lawn, sucking on a blade of grass.

"I hereby call to order today's meeting of the Big Idea Gang," Lizzy stated in a formal voice. "BIG, for short."

"B-I-G," Deon mused. "What else could those letters stand for? Butt—in—"

"Glass!" Connor chirped. "The Butt in Glass Club. I like it."

"Seriously, guys?" Lizzy sighed. "Butt jokes?"

"Boys — Ick — Gross!" Kym groaned. "B-I-G."

Lizzy laughed. She couldn't help herself.

"Guilty as charged!" Connor replied, raising a hand to the sky. "I'm a boy and I'm proud."

"Do you think we should call ourselves a gang?" Kym wondered. "Aren't gangs supposed to be bad?"

"Club might have been a better word," Lizzy admitted. "But BIC doesn't make sense. I thought we needed a *G* word to make a better acronym."

"The Big—Idea—Grapefruit?" Connor offered. He stared at three dumbstruck faces and shrugged. "Okay, another bad idea. Sorry for living."

"So what's the big idea for this week?" Kym asked, trying to get the meeting back on track.

"Well," Lizzy said. "I've been thinking about

the PTA's extra money. Maybe we could come up with a terrific, fabulous, snazzy idea of our own."

"Maybe," Deon said.

"I still want a rocket ship," Connor insisted. Like a bulldog with a bone, Connor wasn't letting go of his big idea.

"Connor," Lizzy said. "You heard Miss Zips. I highly doubt the PTA has that kind of money."

Kym spoke up, "Actually, I was talking with Melanie Cobain—her stepfather's on the PTA—and she says they are thinking about small, inexpensive ideas that can help improve the school."

"Small ideas? Rats! That stinks," Connor blurted.

"Oh, calm down, Connor," Deon said, a little impatiently "The rocket ship is not going to happen."

"I am calm," Connor snapped back, not altogether calmly. He looked down, grumbling to himself.

"Deon is right," Lizzy said, trying to be helpful. "Connor, you don't need a giant hunk of metal when you have your imagination. I've seen you spend three days playing in a big cardboard box."

"I guess," Connor said, sounding unconvinced.

"Besides, I like the idea of little things," Lizzy said. "We could, oh, I don't know, plant a tree!"

"Or expand our community garden!" Kym suggested. She wrote it down in her notebook. "We could grow more vegetables."

"More vegetables, oh joy, that sounds like a blast," Connor groaned.

Kym ignored him. Then she asked, "What about you, Deon? Do you have any ideas?"

Deon sat up. There was a tingling sensation in his belly. For some reason, he felt nervous, uncertain about what he wanted to say. "Well, it's *half* an idea," he explained.

Deon told them about Dinesh, the new boy he met in school. He asked, "I wonder if there's something we could do to, you know, make it easier for him?"

"*Hmmm,*" Lizzy said.

"I've seen that boy," Kym said. "He's the new kid in Mrs. Delgado's class. Do you know him?"

Deon lifted his shoulders and let them drop. "Not really," he said. "It's just that he seems, I don't know, lonely or sad. He's new, you know. He just stands there in the playground, not even doing anything. Recess is supposed to be the best time of the day. And for him it's like . . . a big nothing."

"Maybe he likes being alone," Connor countered. "His idea of fun might be different than yours. Did you ever think of that?"

"It's possible, I suppose," Kym offered.

"Maybe he needs a buddy," Deon said.

"That's your big idea?" Connor frowned. He stood and rubbed his belly. "I'm seriously starving. Anybody want some Doritos?"

Of course, everyone wanted Doritos. They *needed* Doritos. Because that's the way the world works. Human beings need food, air, water, shelter, and Doritos to survive. Everybody knows that.

So Connor went inside the house, leaving Kym alone on one side of the empty bench.

Which prompted Lizzy to say "*Hmmm*" again.

That was two times.

When Lizzy went "*Hmmm*" twice, it usually meant the wheels in her head were going round and round.

"What are you thinking?" Kym asked.

Lizzy cleared her throat. "Have either of you guys ever heard of a buddy bench?"

CHAPTER 7

The Big Idea

Inside the O'Malleys' house, Kym tapped away at the computer keyboard. She began the search by typing in "buddy bench."

Deon and Lizzy stood at her shoulders like human bookends. Connor was nowhere to be seen, probably still foraging in the kitchen like a pig rooting for scraps.

"Cool, check this out." Kym leaned into the screen. She had found an article titled "Kids Don't Have to Be Lonely at Recess Anymore." "This article talks about an ordinary kid who helped spread the idea." She read silently, eyes swiftly scanning the words. Kym turned to Deon. "This

boy gave a presentation to the school board. He even spoke before the whole school."

"But back up," Deon said. "What exactly is a buddy bench, anyway?"

"Look, here's a picture of one," Kym said.

It was a photograph of a bench, painted bright blue. Across the back read the words BUDDY BENCH.

Kym reached for her notebook and started

writing. She scribbled down key words from the article: tolerance, kindness, respect. Kym slid over to another seat so she had more room to write. "Take over at the computer for me, Deon. See what else pops up."

"So if a kid feels lonely or left out, he can sit on the bench and someone will come over," Deon said.

"He *or she*," Kym corrected.

"The bench acts like a signal," Lizzy said. "Everybody needs a buddy."

"Not bad," Deon said. "Write that down, Kym. *Everybody needs a buddy.* That could be our slogan."

At that moment Connor walked past carrying a small stack of Oreos. He paused to glance at the screen, and proceeded to the glass door that opened to the backyard.

"Hey, Con?" Lizzy said. "You should check out what we—"

He stepped out and pulled the door closed without a word.

Meanwhile, Kym and Deon talked excitedly about the buddy benches. "Click on images," Kym suggested.

Deon dragged the mouse and clicked.

"Whoa, look at all of them!" Deon exclaimed. Dozens of photos of brightly painted benches popped up. "Awesome! The PTA should totally do this!"

Lizzy walked to the window. She saw Connor sitting by himself, carefully pulling apart his cookie to get at the creamy filling. "Back in a sec," she said to Deon and Kym.

She went outside to join her twin.

"Mind if I sit with you?" she asked.

Connor shrugged. He was sitting at one end of the long bench.

"So what's up?" Lizzy asked.

"Just bored, I guess," Connor replied.

Lizzy looked up. A cloud drifted in front of the sun. It felt colder. In a month, autumn would turn to winter. Lizzy shivered.

And she waited.

Finally, Connor half mumbled, "Nobody listens to me. You guys all think I'm dumb."

"What are you talking about?" Lizzy asked.

"You know, my rocket ship idea," he replied.

Lizzy suppressed a smile. "Not dumb. But maybe a little unrealistic. Don't you think?"

Connor handed Lizzy his last Oreo. "If I eat all of these, I might hurl," he confessed.

Lizzy took the cookie and, unlike her twin, bit into it without even separating the black exteriors.

Connor shook his head. "You're an animal."

Lizzy grinned and swallowed the rest of the cookie. "Doesn't matter how you eat it, it all goes to the same place."

Connor nodded. "I guess a rocket ship was a pretty bad idea. But you guys didn't even take me seriously."

Lizzy didn't answer. She knew her brother. And she also knew the value of silence.

Connor continued, "I mean, I guess I knew they weren't going to build a rocket ship in the playground. That's got to cost a lot of money. But I've seen them in other places. Like that playground when we were on vacation in Cape Cod. It was awesome! And I thought it would be cool if—"

"It *would* be cool," Lizzy said kindly. "No one's arguing that." She paused before asking, "So what do you think of the buddy bench?"

Connor looked at his sister. "A bench is a good idea," he admitted. "It's kind, too. I wish I thought of it. And besides, just look at us. I was here alone and you came to join me. It works!"

— CHAPTER 8 —

Glitter and Gossip

Miss Zips glided on her fancy black chair with rolling wheels to the front of the room. "I thought we'd start our day by playing with glitter. Everybody likes glitter, right? It's shiny and fun."

The students quickly gathered on the rug. After Miss Zips wisely separated Otis Smick from Bartimus Finkle, she showed the class her personal glitter collection. Miss Zips had a tray with at least a dozen small plastic containers of glitter —gold and blue, bright red and dazzling silver, and more.

"Ooooh," voices murmured.

Miss Zips nodded to Mr. Sanders, who wrote the word GOSSIP on the board. That was when

everyone realized that, despite the glitter, Miss Zips was sharing one of those "teachable moments."

She loved teachable moments.

Rosa Morales whispered to Kym. "Just watch. It starts with glitter. But she's trying to teach us something. Just wait and see." Rosa crossed her arms and sniffed. *Hummphff.*

Kym's eyes never left Miss Zips. She didn't mind a little learning. Kym was not the type of person to speak while Miss Zips was talking. That would be rude. Besides, how was Kym going to become a United States senator if she didn't pay attention in school?

Miss Zips told the class that she was inspired to try this activity because of all the wild talk about the PTA's extra money. "There were a lot of stories and rumors going around. All that loose talk reminded me of gossip," Miss Zips said. She looked around the room. "Would anyone like to tell me what that word means?"

Suri Brewster's hand shot to the ceiling. "Gossip is when people say things about other people that might be hurtful or untrue."

"Very good, Suri," Miss Zips said. "That's exactly right. Gossip often involves rumors or information that hasn't been confirmed as true. When we don't know the facts, it's often best to keep our mouths shut."

The class listened quietly. Some of them stared at the rug. Others fiddled with the Velcro on their shoes. They secretly hoped that Miss Zips would get back to the glitter.

"Mr. Sanders," said Miss Zips. "Do you happen to have any money in your pocket?"

The classroom aide reluctantly lifted a twenty-dollar bill from his wallet.

"Now we'll play a little game," Miss Zips said. "I'll need five volunteers."

The twenty-dollar bill inspired a lot of class participation. Everyone raised a hand, and some students raised both hands. Miss Zips selected Kym, Hayden, Kaylee, Connor, and Padma Bitar to stand in the front of the room.

Everyone else moaned in disappointment.

"Don't worry, I promise you'll all get a turn," Miss Zips said. "For now, I have a simple task for our five volunteers to complete." She poured glitter into Kym's hands. "All you have to do is pass it along down the line. When you accomplish that, I'll gladly give you this twenty dollars."

"Hey!" Mr. Sanders protested.

Miss Zips held up a finger. "However, not one speck of glitter is allowed to fall to the floor, or stick to your hands. You have to pass it along perfectly. Okay? You have three minutes. Go!"

Well, the students tried. They really did. But it was an impossible task. And it got more impossible, and a bit soggier, after Connor sneezed. *Yuck.* By the end of three minutes, glitter was spilled everywhere. No matter how careful the students were, pieces stuck to everyone's hands. Bits sprinkled to the floor. Different groups of five teamed up, but not one succeeded. After everyone tried and failed, Miss Zips asked if the

class had learned anything. "Yeah, I'm never going to be a millionaire," Deon muttered.

Giggles filled the room.

Kym said, "I think you were trying to tell us that gossip is like glitter."

Miss Zips nodded. "Gossip sticks to people, even when it's not true. And sometimes our gossip travels to places we never intended for it to go. Gossip seems sparkly and fun in the beginning —but it usually ends up making a mess."

Mr. Sanders stepped forward to gently pluck the twenty-dollar bill from Miss Zips's hand. "Let's hope this money sticks to me," he chuckled.

Miss Zips smiled. "I'm glad Mr. Sanders is happy. And I have news that I think will make our entire class happy, too."

"Real news or fake news?" Connor asked.

"The best kind of news, direct from the source," Miss Zips replied. "According to Principal Tuxbury, the PTA has indeed raised quite a bit of money this year. And they are going to use that money to help the school."

A chorus of cheers filled the room.

Lizzy raised a hand.

"Thank you for not calling out, Lizzy," Miss Zips said. "Did you have a comment?"

"Well, a question, really," Lizzy replied. "Did they decide what to buy?"

Miss Zips nodded. "Yes, the PTA made a decision last night."

Deon's shoulders slumped. His body sagged. *The PTA has already decided?* He didn't even get a chance to tell anybody about his idea.

CHAPTER 9

The Art of Persuasion

Miss Zips leaned forward in her chair. "The PTA has made a generous gift to our library. Ms. Ronson, our librarian, will use those funds to purchase books for the school." Miss Zips smiled from ear to ear. "Isn't that wonderful?"

Everyone in class seemed to think so.

Except for one person.

Deon was quietly devastated.

Miss Zips let the class take a snack break before heading down to the music room. Out came the strawberries and the Goldfish, the rice balls and mini bagels and diced mangos.

Lizzy felt disappointed, naturally. But she had smiled back at Miss Zips. Lizzy realized that books were important. She couldn't possibly complain about books. Kym was thrilled. The idea of books filled her insides with tiny, happy bubbles, as if she were a human bottle of sparkling seltzer. She gushed to Lizzy, "I could just burst with happiness. Books, fabulous books!"

Meanwhile, Connor stared at his best friend.

Deon seemed to shrink before Connor's eyes. It was like watching the air slowly leak out of a balloon.

Connor patted his pal on the back. "Don't feel bad, D," he said.

Deon grumbled, "I never got a chance. My big idea just went *poof.*"

Connor looked at Deon in surprise. He jabbed a finger against the desk. "So that's it? Poof? You're giving up?"

"You heard Miss Zips," Deon replied. "It's already been decided."

"But you have a really good idea," Connor said. "A terrific idea. You can't give up now."

Deon's eyes flickered for a moment. Then he shook his head, defeated. "It's over."

"It's ain't over till it's over," Connor said. "At least that's what my father tells me. We can't give up. Think about Dinesh." At those words, Connor strode to Miss Zips's desk. In seconds, he was waving his arms, speaking a mile a minute. He turned and gestured for Deon to come over. "Tell her about the buddy bench," Connor said.

So Deon began to talk. And Miss Zips listened. *She really listened.* Deon talked about Dinesh, and the playground, and making the school a better place for everyone. Soon Lizzy and Kym joined the conversation. After Deon was through, Miss Zips sat nodding her head. Her eyes sparkled like sunlight on the water. "Well, you've convinced me, Deon. It's a wonderful idea."

"Thanks," Deon said. "But it will never—"

"Never say never," Miss Zips said, grinning. "You can't give up on a really good idea."

"But what do I do?" Deon asked.

"It's time for you to practice the fine art of persuasion," Miss Zips said.

"Persuasion?" Lizzy repeated.

"Yes," Miss Zips replied. "You have to convince others of your opinion—just like you convinced me. Deon spoke with real emotion. He tugged at my heart."

"I did?" Deon asked.

"Deon, when you say you want to make the school better, what do you mean by *better?*" Miss Zips asked.

Deon blinked.

Kym ventured a guess. "Kinder? Gentler?"

"Yes," Miss Zips said, clapping her hands together. "Those are good words."

"We've done lots of research," Lizzy said.

Kym remembered the key words from the article she had written in her notes: tolerance, kindness, respect.

"So what's the problem?" Miss Zips asked.

"There are two problems," Connor said. "First, no money. And second, how are we going to talk to the PTA? We're just kids."

Miss Zips tilted her head this way and that. "Keep thinking. Keep working on your argument," she said. "You've already done the hard part."

"We have?" Connor said.

"Yes, you've already come up with a beautiful, wonderful, terrific idea. Now you need to sell it to the people in charge."

Kym tapped a finger against her lips. Her eyes narrowed. "If only we knew somebody . . . who knew somebody . . . who was on the PTA." Her head swiveled toward the reading rug. Connor, Lizzy, Deon, and Miss Zips followed Kym's gaze to where one girl in pointy glasses demonstrated a series of dance moves to her friends.

"Ah, Suri Brewster," Lizzy said.

CHAPTER 10

The New Librarian

Lizzy suggested that the Big Idea Gang meet the next afternoon in the school library after the last bell. "Instead of going straight home, we can meet to do more research on the buddy bench. Just because the PTA has decided to spend the money on books, we shouldn't give up on our idea," she reasoned.

"My mom can pick us up," Deon offered. "She loves driving everyone all over creation."

"Really?" Kym asked.

"That's what she says," Deon said. Then he paused, thinking it over. "Maybe she *grumbles* it."

"Oh, sarcastically," Lizzy said. "That's when you say the opposite of what you mean."

Deon tugged on his ear. Lizzy had a point. He'd try to remember to thank his mom when she picked them up.

The library was a large, well-lit room with low bookshelves and long tables. It had neat nooks and crannies, too—little alcoves with comfy chairs for peaceful reading.

Mrs. Buckminster had been the librarian at Clay Elementary forever. She used to joke that she'd been at Clay since before the dinosaurs. That wasn't exactly true, but it seemed almost believable. That's why it felt so strange when she retired and a zippy new librarian, Ms. Sasha Ronson, took her place.

Ms. Ronson didn't look much older than most middle-schoolers. Small and thin, she wore her hair short and dyed bright red at the tips. Ms. Ronson was young and energetic. She wore colorful scarves and six earrings in each ear. She even had tattoos. And, of course, the kids loved her immediately—mostly because of her lively personality.

Lizzy sat at the table with the others. Padma Bitar and her friend, Maggie Uggums, studied together at a nearby table. The assistant librarian, Mrs. Jaffe-Klein, pecked away at the computer, her long nails tap-tap-tapping on the keyboard. Ms. Ronson was crouched on the rug, energetically pulling random books off the low shelves and stacking them in piles. She seemed to be muttering to herself.

Lizzy stared at a blank sheet of paper. Suddenly all her previous enthusiasm seemed to drain out of her. It seemed too hard. The PTA had decided to buy books. Lizzy looked around the library. She loved books. How could she persuade the PTA to spend money on something else?

She noticed that Padma, one of the best artists in the entire school, was sketching on a pad. Lizzy walked over to take a look. "What are you drawing?" she asked.

Padma had a long, thick, black ponytail. She looked up at Lizzy. "I'm supposed to be doing homework. But I got inspired. Do you like it?"

"I do, but will there be colors?" Lizzy asked.

"Oh yes," Padma said. "This is a pencil sketch for a big painting I just dreamed up." Padma gestured with her hands, pressing them like a mime against an imaginary wall. "I was thinking I could fill a canvas, or a wall, with handprints using a rainbow of colors."

"*Hmmm,*" said Lizzy.

She was getting the beginning of an idea. Just

the tiniest flicker of something—like a small fish glittering in the vast sea—stirred deep inside Lizzy's brain.

Lizzy put her hands in her front pockets. She shifted her weight from foot to foot. The buddy bench was a great idea—but maybe it needed a little help.

And, hey, maybe it wouldn't cost so much after all.

"Excuse me, Lizzy? Padma?" a voice called. It was Ms. Ronson, now on her hands and knees by a back bookshelf. "Could you please bring over those boxes? Thanks ever so much."

Ms. Ronson dumped some of the books in the first box. "Good riddance," she muttered.

Lizzy was alarmed. "What are you doing? You can't throw away books! It's a waste of money."

"Oh, Lizzy," Ms. Ronson said, "some of these books have been here forever. No one reads them. They are taking up valuable space. Look at this book." The young librarian held up an old science book. The cover read FUN WITH COMPUTERS!

"This book is twenty years old. It's terribly out of date. It's useless, Lizzy, and it's got to go."

Lizzy could see that Ms. Ronson was right.

"Here's another," Ms. Ronson said, her voice rising. The cover read CAREERS FOR WOMEN. Ms. Ronson flipped through the stale, yellowed pages. "Look at these jobs. Secretary, flight attendant, piano teacher, bank teller!" Ms. Ronson actually growled, *grrrrr*. "Where's scientist? Or financial analyst? Or astronaut? Or how about president? Maybe that's what our country needs —a woman in the White House!"

The book sailed through the air, as if its pages were wings, and landed into the box marked TRASH.

Ms. Ronson laughed. "I'm sorry, it just makes me crazy." She swept an arm across the room. "Our graphic novel section is much too small. I can't keep enough scary books on the shelves, because they are so popular. I don't have any of this year's new award winners. Libraries have to change with the times. This is why it's so wonderful that the PTA has decided to donate money for books. Don't you agree?"

Lizzy and Padma nodded. Yes, they sure did. Lizzy tugged on Padma's arm. "Come with me," she whispered. "I want you to talk with the rest of the gang. I think I've got an idea—but we'll need your help."

— CHAPTER 11 —

Deon and Dinesh

Mrs. Gibson pulled a silver minivan up to the front doors. Deon sat in the front passenger seat, while Connor, Kym, and Lizzy climbed into the back with a big posterboard. It read EVERYBODY NEEDS A BUDDY across the top and had a drawing of a bench with Padma's colorful handprint design all over it.

"So what was the Big Idea Gang up to this afternoon?" Mrs. Gibson asked.

They told her all about the PTA buying new books for the library and their idea for the buddy bench.

"I was ready to give up," Deon admitted. He shot a look toward the back seat. "But Connor wouldn't let me."

"We decided to try harder," Kym said.

"One big problem was the money," Lizzy said. "Then I realized we had an old bench in our backyard. If the PTA could donate money, my family could donate an old bench."

"You might want to check with your parents first," Mrs. Gibson said.

"Already did," Lizzy said, beaming.

"And this girl in our school, Padma, she's, like,

x

70

an amazing artist," Connor jumped in. "She's going to help us paint the bench—for free."

"We still need to convince the PTA," Kym said. "But we have a connection. Our friend Suri said we can come over tonight to share our idea. Her mother is treasurer for the PTA. If she likes the buddy bench, she can bring it up at the next meeting."

Ms. Gibson glanced in the rearview mirror. "I'm so glad to hear about this project. This is an opportunity to make a difference right here in your own community. This is how positive change happens. With kids like you."

"I'm positive we'll get our buddy bench," Connor said.

"What makes you so sure?" Kym asked.

"I'm wearing my lucky underwear," Connor explained.

Kym gagged as if she'd just swallowed bad fish. "Ew, gross," she groaned.

"What's the matter?" Connor asked. "You don't have lucky underwear?"

"Seriously? No," Kym stated. She looked ill.

Lizzy rubbed the temples of her forehead. She apologized to Deon's mother, "He's my twin brother, but some days I wonder if he wandered over from a petting zoo."

"What color is it?" Deon asked.

"Sort of aqua green," Connor said. "It's a happy color. Do you want to—"

"NO!" Mrs. Gibson said, waving a hand, laughing. "I'm shutting down this conversation. Please, no more talk about underwear."

"But—"

"No!" Mrs. Gibson repeated. "No buts."

No one said a peep. Finally, Deon asked in a soft voice, "So . . . just to be clear, Mom. We can't talk about butts either?"

It was that kind of car ride.

After dropping everyone off, Mrs. Gibson and Deon drove home in silence. Deon thought about Dinesh Barazani. They had talked a little bit over the past couple of days. Dinesh was very quiet, but he was slowly beginning to trust Deon.

Dinesh told Deon that he was from Pakistan. He liked math and video games. His English was very good, but very fast. He told Deon he grew up speaking two languages in his home—English and something called Urdu. His father came to America for a job in the hospital. He was a heart surgeon.

Deon explained to his mother how Dinesh had inspired their big idea. "I don't know if a buddy bench will solve the problem," Deon said.

"But every single day I smile at him. I figure that everybody likes a smile."

"I'm proud of you, Deon," Mrs. Gibson reached a hand to Deon's knee and gave it a squeeze. "The buddy bench is great idea. I'm positive the school is going to love it."

"How are you sure?" Deon asked. "Are you wearing your lucky underwear, too?"

Mrs. Gibson looked at her son . . . and winked.

CHAPTER 12

The Best Part

In the end, the school didn't take the O'Malleys' bench for the playground. Instead, they purchased two brand-new buddy benches—one for each end of the playground—because they loved Deon's idea so much.

They got a local carpenter, one of the parents at the school, to build the benches. Padma supervised the painting. So one afternoon, a bunch of kids and teachers came together to finish the project. Everyone had a hand in the painting.

At first, the students at Clay Elementary were really excited about the new benches. There was even a long, scraggly line of kids eager to sit on them. But after a few days, life on the playground returned to normal. Boys and girls ran around

like lunatics. They needed to jump and scream and shout. But on the day after Moses Federman's cat, Puddles, died of liver failure, Moses felt downhearted. So he sat on the bench and waited for someone to come along.

"Want to play?" Lizzy asked.

Moses shook his head, eyes moist. "Not really."

"How about a walk and talk?" Lizzy offered. "Or, you know, I could just sit here with you if that's okay?"

And so she did.

Moses felt a little better after that.

On the fourth day, Dinesh took a seat at the bench. Deon was ready. This was the moment he'd been waiting for. But as he walked toward the bench, a curly-haired boy beat him to it. Deon watched as the two of them went off together. They climbed to the top of the geodesic dome, sat close together, and talked. Deon felt disappointed at first. The buddy bench was his idea, after all. Without even thinking about it,

Deon walked to the empty bench and plopped down.

A minute later, there was Connor, holding a basketball. "Dude, you wanna?"

Deon smiled at his friend. "Oh yeah I do!"

They raced off together, passing the ball between them, because, after all, recess was absolutely, positively, 100 percent, totally the best part of the school day.

Why?

Because that's when boys and girls got together with their friends. The tall ones and the short ones . . . the shy ones and the wild ones . . . the ones with blonde hair and brown and black. All of them, mixed up together like crayons in a box.

Everybody needs a buddy.

Just ask Deon Gibson. He'll tell you.

Miss Zips's "Wow Me" Tips

So you want to make a difference? That's great! There are so many ways that you can make a difference in your school, your community, and even the world! But making things better means making changes, and you'll need to convince people that those changes are worth making.

A logical argument is the best way to get others to see your point of view, because you are giving them reasons to be persuaded. Let's start at the beginning.

What's the big idea?

Presenting an argument is not about being the loudest, or the funniest, or even the smartest. As I tell my students all the time, it's about making a claim and supporting that claim with evidence.

What do you need to convince your audience of? A claim often starts with a big idea. An idea is "big" if it is something you feel excited or passionate about. If you don't feel strongly, how can you convince anyone else to agree with you?

Deon had the big idea that Clay Elementary should get a buddy bench. To turn that idea into a claim, the BIG needed to be specific, direct, and make one main point: a buddy bench would be a positive addition to Clay Elementary to help students connect with each other and encourage kindness and inclusion. There is no question about what they are arguing!

Now what? Support that claim!

Supporting your claim means trying to prove it. Think about it this way: if you simply made a claim and stopped there, your audience would be left wondering, WHY? So you have to answer that question for them. You have to give your audience reasons to be persuaded, and back those reasons up with evidence such as facts and details.

It's always good to start by asking yourself some questions. For example:

- **What are the benefits of getting a buddy bench?**

- **Is there another way to help students connect and make newcomers feel welcome without it?**

- **What are possible obstacles to getting a buddy bench, and how can I argue against them?**

Being able to answer these kinds of questions will give you the reasons for your argument and help you come up with the facts and details you need to support your claim.

Let's look at Deon's argument. What support does he offer to convince the Clay Elementary PTA to approve a buddy bench?

REASON: A buddy bench will help lonely students connect and make new students feel welcome.

EVIDENCE: Deon has noticed a shy new student, Dinesh Barazani, standing alone at recess, and wants to find an accessible way to make him feel more included.

REASON: A buddy bench will not cost the PTA any funds to provide.

EVIDENCE: Lizzy and Connor's parents will donate a bench for free, and Padma will paint it for free as well.

Wrap it up!

Now that you've made your claim and supported it with reasons and evidence, it's time to wrap everything up in the conclusion of your argument.

This is your last chance to get your audience to agree with your point of view—make the most of it! In your conclusion, you can restate your claim, tie up any loose ends, and make a call to action if needed. A call to action asks your audience to believe something or do something. The BIG creates a slogan: "Everybody needs a buddy!" This is a call to action because they are asking the school to support the idea of a buddy bench.

Put it all together!

What we've just gone over are the basic elements of a strong argument. This is a good format to follow for your next persuasive speech, writing assignment, or anytime you want to be convincing. Now you have all the tools you need to take that first step toward making a difference.

So, what's *your* big idea? Better get to work— you've got a lot of convincing to do, and I want you to wow me!